I'M ONLY LITTLE

ONLY

BY ME!

as told to Roger Hargreaves

A Thurman Book

PRICE/STERN/SLOAN
Publishers, Ltd., London

Hello! I'm Mr Small.

I really am very little.

How little?

Well!

About as big as your little finger!

That's without my hat on, of course!

I live in a tiny house under a daisy at the bottom of Mr Robinson's garden.

I quite often walk up to see Mr Robinson.

He's a good friend.

It takes nearly all day to go there and back, because with short legs you can only take short steps.

I went to see him last Wednesday after breakfast.

One cornflake.

One drop of milk.

Five grains of sugar.

And a crumb.

With a dab of butter and a spot of marmalade.

That's quite a big breakfast for me!

As I walked up the garden path I met a worm.

"Hello," I said, raising my hat. "Isn't it cold today?"

"Isn't what cold today?" sniffed the worm.

Worms are like that!

When I arrived at Mr Robinson's I was quite exhausted, and very cold.

I used to knock at his door, but that never used to work. You see, my loudest knock is still a very quiet knock, and Mr Robinson never used to hear it.

So he tied a piece of cotton to his letterbox, and now, when I pull the cotton, the letterbox rattles, and Mr Robinson can hear that.

I reached up and pulled the piece of cotton.

Oh, dear!

I pulled so hard, it snapped!

What was I to do?

Then I heard footsteps.

I jumped hastily out of the way.

When you're as little as I am, you can't be too careful!

It was the postman!

I thought I'd seen him somewhere before.

"Excuse me,"
I piped. "Could
you press the
doorbell for me
please?"

"Hello, there,
Mr Small,"
grinned the
postman as he
pressed the bell.

Mr Robinson came to the door.

"Letter for you," said the postman.

"And," he added, "a friend to see you."

"A friend?" asked Mr Robinson looking around. "Where?"

"Here!" I shouted.

You try shouting "Here!" in your littlest whisper.

Go on!

Try it!

That's about as loud as my shout.

But, Mr Robinson heard it.

"Hello, Mr Small," smiled Mr Robinson.

"Hello," I yelled.

The postman gave Mr Robinson the letter, and off he went.

Mr Robinson picked me up, carefully, and took me into the kitchen.

"Coffee?" he suggested.

"Lovely," I replied.

And he poured one drop of coffee into a very, very tiny cup.

His daughter had found it in a doll's house and had given it to him.

For me!

"Pull up a chair," he said.

And I sat down, on top of the kitchen table, in MY chair!

Mr Robinson had made it specially for me out of five and half matchsticks!

"Who's the letter from?" I asked.

"We won't know until we open it, will we?" Mr Robinson chuckled.

Mr Robinson opened the envelope, and read the letter.

And then he read it again.

"Gosh!" he said. "I've been invited to go to a university in California for a whole year!"

Mr Robinson is a professor.

My heart sank.

"Congratulations," I said.

"You don't look very happy about it," remarked Mr Robinson.

"Well," I said, "I'll miss you!"

"Hmm," he said, stroking his chin.

He thought for a moment.

"How would you like to come with me?" he said.

"Me?" I said.

"Yes," he said. "You!"

I was so excited!

I got back to the bottom of Mr Robinson's garden in record time.

"I'm off to California!" I shouted to the worm as I ran past him.

"When?" he sniffed.

"In the morning!" I cried.

I spent most of the rest of the day packing.

Getting to sleep in my little bed that night was very difficult.

But the morning dawned, and off we set.

Me and Mr Robinson.

Mr Robinson and I.

Both of us.

And so here I am one week later!

In sunny California!

On a Wednesday afternoon.

Sitting by my swimming pool.

Writing this book.

Gosh!

The sun is hot!

Much hotter than at home!

Actually, I think I should explain about the swimming pool.

The university have lent Mr Robinson a house, and the house has a pool.

But, I don't dare to go in it!

It's a hundred times deeper than little old me!

And that's at the shallow end!

So Mr Robinson came up with a very good idea.

He went to the supermarket and came home with a brand-new dog bowl.

It makes a very good swimming pool.

And you need a pool when it's as hot as this!

Ah!

This is the life!

Sitting in the sun!

Writing my book!

Sitting in the sun!

Taking a dip!

And, sitting in the sun!

Actually, I think I'll go and finish this book inside now.

Gosh!

I've just looked in the mirror!

Oh, dear!

I think I've spent too much time sitting in the sun!

I've gone all red!